CAROLINE
AT THE KING'S BALL

by Jean le Paillot   pictures by Florence

Parents' Magazine Press/New York

CAROLINE the cow was taking the evening air when she saw Anne passing by. The little girl was wearing a pretty white dress and her mother had curled her hair.

"Hello, Anne," said the cow.
"Hello, Caroline," replied Anne.
"Where are you going all dressed up?"
"I am going to dance at the king's ball."

"What a pity I wasn't invited," thought the cow as Anne went on her way. "But after all, why can't I go to the king's ball? People of my rank don't need invitations!"

The cow opened the farmer's wife's closet. On special occasions, the farmer's wife and Caroline lent each other their clothes. The cow chose a beautiful red gown, a large red hat with mauve ribbons, and a magnificent blue parasol. She cut two holes in the hat for her horns and added two clusters of curls. Then she pinned a large cauliflower on her gown and powdered her nose with flour. Looking at herself in the mirror, she decided she looked positively charming.

When the servant who announced the guests at the king's ball saw Caroline arrive in her red gown, her red hat with its mauve ribbons and her curls, he was so impressed that he didn't dare to ask for her invitation. And so the cow entered the king's ballroom.

It was very different from the farmer's yard with its turkeys and chickens! There were countesses, duchesses, princesses—it was truly a royal court. All these beautiful people chattered and walked about on the marble floor. The cow admired everything and everybody.

A servant offered her orangeade and lemonade.

"No, thank you," she said. "I'd like a bucket of water, please."

Another servant offered her sandwiches or crackers or cakes.

"No, thank you," she said. "I'd like a bale of hay, please."

They brought her the bucket of water and the bale of hay, and the cow sat down in an easy chair in the green salon, munching on the hay and sipping the water through a straw.

In the main hall, people were dancing waltzes and polkas. But no one asked the cow to dance—not a count, nor a duke nor a prince, and the cow was very sad.

The master of ceremonies, who was in charge of the invitations, was an unpleasant man. He said, "There's a cow with a red hat in the green salon, and there's no such person on my guest list!"

Caroline was dancing all alone, the hay under her arm and the bucket in her hoof. Spinning around on her toes, she closed her eyes so that she could enjoy the sensation of twirling much better.

"Cow, cow! You're having a fine time now, but trouble's coming!" cried Anne, very much upset. In fact, the master of ceremonies was pointing his finger at Caroline.

"Aha! You have come to the king's ball without an invitation! Guards, take this cow to prison!"

The guards surrounded Caroline.

"Throw me in prison! What a laugh! Then there will be no more cheese for the king!" replied the cow.

Caroline made the best cheese in the country. When the king heard the word "cheese" he said, "What's your name, cow?"

"Caroline, Your Majesty," she replied, with a curtsy.

"Caroline? Is it you who makes those marvelous cheeses?"

"It certainly is, Your Majesty!"

"I am very happy to see you, Caroline! Come, let's dance." The king led Caroline into the ballroom. Whether or not she had an invitation no longer mattered, and the master of ceremonies was very much annoyed.

"What a beautiful cauliflower you are wearing," the king said to Caroline. "Would you like me to make you a princess?"

"No, Your Majesty. But tell me, why are none of my cheeses being served at your ball?"

"Because I keep them all for myself," the king said, embarrassed.

Caroline's eyes widened when she heard that. To make her forget his greediness, the king danced three waltzes and four polkas with her. Everyone wanted to dance with her after the king did. She wrote their names on her dance card and said to them, "You must wait your turn. I will be back to you for the fifth dance..."

Finally, she said, "I only have one dance left to offer. But to make it up to those I can't dance with, I shall give them some of my cheese."

All those who couldn't dance with Caroline received a box of her marvelous cheese.

She danced until dawn and drank a bucket of water with some grenadine in it.

Her head was spinning a little when she returned home, singing

. . . et ron et zon,
mon petit gazon.

The next day her cheese smelled of the party. People whispered, "Caroline is happy because she went to the king's ball."

"Why didn't you want to be a princess, cow?" asked Anne.

"It's hard to be a princess and a cow at the same time," Caroline explained, "and it's better to be a good cow of the king's than a bad queen of the cows!"

JEAN LE PAILLOT is actually Georges Van Hout, a mathematician and logician who has published a number of scholarly works in these fields. It is under the name of Jean le Paillot that he is a drama critic, theater director and has adapted Greek and Shakespearian plays for the French theater as well as for radio and television. He has also worked extensively in children's theater as a teacher, director and author.

Mr. Van Hout states that he first began telling stories of Caroline the cow to encourage his young daughter to eat her vegetable soup. Since this little girl has now grown up to become a doctor, Mr. Van Hout hopes that all young children will read the Caroline stories, eat their vegetable soup and grow up to be doctors, too.

FLORENCE (Maria Wabbes) has illustrated over fifteen books for children. She also designs textiles for children's wear and collaborates on a special page for children in the newspaper, *Le Soir*. Her home is a country house in a small Belgian village where she is surrounded by all kinds of animals—horses, dogs, cats and even a real cow named Caroline. She is the wife of a well-known interior designer and the mother of five children.

When Georges Van Hout told a story of Caroline on a radio program for children, Mrs. Wabbes was so intrigued that she immediately contacted him, eager to do the illustrations. And thus Caroline the cow became the subject of a series of picture books.